"4 Fun Flavors!"

Written by Dustin Lewit

Table of Contents:

1) Quicksand

2) Possession Is Nine-Tenths Of The Law

3) A Conniving Neurosurgeon And His Patient Atop A Ferris Wheel At A Carnival For Atheists

4) The Safe

Quicksand

The cement was being poured into the quicksand rapidly devouring alive Harold Careful.

"Why are you doing this to me?" Harold asked, mouth chewing on quicksand.

"I have my orders." the person pouring the cement said.

Eventually, the cement hardened and poor Harold Careful was buried alive without a chance of being rescued.

Now we will rewind to find out what Harold Careful did to deserve being buried alive in quicksand and cement.

Harold got his last name because, for majority of his life, he played things cautiously. That's why everyone associated with Mr. Cautious were dumbstruck at learning what he did for a living:

"Racecar driver?! That's very out of character, Harold!" everyone who knew him said.

Harold had Saturdays off, so he went out

showing off his custom dual-engine 1,000 mph top speed Mr. Careful-brand race car.

A woman flashing her many degrees of higher education distracted Harold's eyes from the road. He lost control of the car and flipped it on top of the wife of an extremely powerful man.

When the extremely powerful man heard about who was responsible for his woman's grisly end, he ordered some friends he knew in low places to kidnap Harold Careful, place him in quicksand, and finish the avengement of the extremely powerful man's wife with cement.

It surprised the extremely powerful man to see that Harold Careful punched through the hardened cement and escaped.

"Harold Careful is a far more powerful man than I!" the extremely powerful man wept.

If you didn't believe in karma before, perhaps now will end your reign of cynicism making you believe that nothing going around ever comes around.

Harold Careful, while escaping, was destroyed by a bus. He survived, but was severely disfigured.

Gimping around on his two snapped apart legs, Harold found himself face down in a forest. A stick poking him in his neck woke him up.

It was a headless body holding flash cards as its main form of communication.

"Are you alright?" a flash card read, held on a pole where neck and skull should've been.

"I was destroyed by a bus, but am somehow alive." Harold Careful wrote down on the flash card handed to him by the headless helper. The headless good soul had a pencil handy, too.

"How can a headless person read flash cards?" Harold asked.

The headless person pulled a sword out of their cape, decapitating Harold Careful. Of course, the headless person had surgical knowledge about sewing heads onto headless bodies.

After the headless person stitched Harold Careful's head to itself, it decided to get out of the forest and hang out on the adjoining beach.

The extremely powerful man asked anybody and everybody he came in contact with:

"Have you seen this guy?" as he held a photograph of Harold Careful looking like a perverted Prince Charming. His fingers were shaped as a "V" and his tongue wagged madly in the middle.

"Yeah. He was walking around at the beach scaring the shit out of all the drunks and stoners with that surgical shit on his neck." one pedestrian told the extremely powerful man.

"Where could I talk with these beach people?"

the extremely powerful man asked.

"The beach, but I'd take caution. Rumor is spreading that this guy in your photograph has been making anyone who looks at him strangely disappear in the beach sand. Like…" the pedestrian giving invaluable information to the extremely powerful man began.

"Like what?" the extremely powerful man asked, patience thinner than an anorexic.

"Quicksand." the pedestrian said, then dropped into the solid concrete where he stood.

Observing this absurd phenomenon, the extremely powerful man noted:

"It's as if Harold Careful has the otherworldly ability to…"

"Make anyone I so desire disappear like quicksand?" Harold Careful's head was told to say by the once headless body.

"If this is about what I did to you…I want you to know I'd do it again, with orgasmic pleasure. You killed my wife, Mr. Careful." the extremely powerful man said, postured proudly. "So drop me in quicksand, carve me up and put me on a deli rack. I truly don't care about living after you took the only person who every really loved me away."

Harold Careful's head began crying. The body it was attached to didn't understand this human emotion.

"Rebury me in quicksand and cement. I deserve my punishment." Harold Careful's head said. The body it was stitched to began flailing in frustration over lack of situational control.

Noticing the fear in the extremely powerful

man's eyes at the unpredictability of the body

possessing Harold Careful, Harold sadly laughed:

"The body doesn't want what the mind wants."

The extremely powerful man threw Harold

Careful in quicksand and cement, saluting Harold as

he disappeared permanently.

<u>Possession Is Nine-Tenths Of The Law</u>

Mr. Rummage Sale fell into a grave freshly dug for someone else.

"Mr. Rummage Sale, get out of that hole!" the carnival barker hired to hype the cemetery said.

"Possession is nine-tenths of the law. I'm not paying for any wood for any coffin and I sure as Hell am not paying for six feet of God's land. You get started on digging another hole. I'm staying here until I die." Mr. Rummage Sale said.

"Get out of that grave!" the 300 members of the deceased person's family said.

From inside the casket, the deceased was furious about having to rot above ground waiting for this asshole:

"Look, pal. I know I'm dead and all, but I paid a fortune for this plot. In fact, I died broke."

All 300 members of the deceased's family got up and left. They said to Mr. Rummage Sale as they dumped out their dead from his casket:

"Keep the grave and here's a complementary casket."

A Conniving Neurosurgeon And His Patient Atop A Ferris Wheel At A Carnival For Atheists

At the top of the Ferris wheel, a neurosurgeon and his patient were opening each others heads and handing each other their brains. From a distance, it seemed like an even exchange. Up close, the neurosurgeon kept his brain but took his patient's.

Kicking the patient 100-200 feet in the air, the neurosurgeon bids farewell with:

"Now you're a politician!"

The patient responded, in mid-air, with:

"No, you are the politician for you have stolen from me!"

The brain-less patient lay smoked on carnival ground.

"Thank God for waivers of liability!" the neurosurgeon said from atop the Ferris wheel.

"Did he thank GOD?!" the visitors of the carnival asked, outraged like exaggerated cartoon characters.

"This is an atheist convention!" someone in the crowd explained to the neurosurgeon.

"You're all nuts! I am an atheist too! I am a man of science, not biblical fairy tales!" the neurosurgeon tried to save his ass with.

A laser cutter mystifyingly appeared from the sky. It sliced open the neurosurgeon's head, causing his brain to fall on carnival ground.

Miraculously, the brain-less patient got up from where he was believed to have died and walked over to where the neurosurgeon's brain was nearby. He put the brain into his open head and asked for a stapler.

"We believe!" the atheists said. "By God, we believe!"

The carnival manager, mouth open like a draw-bridge, said:

"I believe in making an Almighty amount of money off of what has transpired here!"

The carnival manager mystifyingly caught fire.

The Safe

Ski masked 7 foot 8 men. Two man job involving the theft of a safe. Late at night.

"I heard something screaming in this thing." Ski Masked 7 foot 8 Man, the first, said.

"Turn off that imagination of yours." Ski Masked 7 foot 8 Man, the second, said. "I only hear my heart rate elevated to tachycardia territory. Why couldn't I get a respectable occupation?"

"Employers frown on jail birds, even after they

leave the nest." Ski Masked 7 foot 8 Man, the first, explained as if he were lecturing a two year old.

Both ski masked 7 foot 8 men heard the screaming coming from within the safe. Frightened, they dropped all six tons of steel.

The safe opened by itself…

A face with child-like qualities stares at the ski masked 7 foot 8 men…

"Who would lock such a precious child in a filthy seventy year old safe?" both ski masked 7 foot

8 men ask…

The child-like face turns into a blistered wreck of an old demonic man.

"Oh, now we understand." the two ski masked 7 foot 8 men said as the hideous creature within the safe ate their eyeballs.

"Get out of my house!" the awful-looking freak said as it jumped out of the safe, running into the kitchen.

Through the kitchen window, as the monster was

grabbing for straws to drink the thieves' blood with, a

police officer with a high powered rifle across the

street told his ear piece authority:

"I have target locked."

"Execute. After 150 years of waiting for this

fucker to come out of that Goddamned safe, shoot to

kill!" the police officer's authority said.

The monster was shot in the throat. Watching the

little bastard grab its throat and drop dead made the

police officer laugh intensely.

THE END

Thank you for choosing me to be your

entertainment!

9 798843 782542